LINCOLN LIVES LARGE

Written by
Megan Troka

AuthorHouse™
1663 Liberty Drive
Bloomington, IN 47403
www.authorhouse.com
Phone: 1 (800) 839-8640

Published by AuthorHouse 10/15/2018

ISBN: 978-1-5462-6414-9 (sc)
ISBN: 978-1-5462-6415-6 (hc)
ISBN: 978-1-5462-6413-2 (e)

Library of Congress Control Number: 2018912273

Print information available on the last page.

This book is printed on acid-free paper.

authorHOUSE®

This book is dedicated to
ALL dogs, dog lovers and
my Lincoln.

You take up 90% of the bed, drool everywhere, and demand
constant attention. I wouldn't have it any other way. Thank
you for your constant friendship, snuggles and for teaching
me a thing or two about patience.

Keep living large Lincoln!

Little baby Lincoln could fit in a shoe,
but that didn't last long, soon he grew, grew, grew.

When he stood on his back legs he was 7 feet high.
A dog so large he could almost touch the sky.

Being large does not come with ease.
Lincoln's first time at the dog park left some unpleased.

Upon arriving Lincoln raced through the gates.
Slow down Lincoln, that's too fast a pace!

To avoid being trampled the dogs leapt out of his way.
He'd better be mindful of his size if he plans to stay.

After that sprint, Lincoln wanted a drink.
Slurp Slurp Slurp
Other dogs needed water too, but Lincoln didn't think.
Slurp Slurp Slurp

At empty bowls Lincoln stared,
while the thirsty dogs stood by and glared.

The sun was beating down making the day too hot.
Where could a dog cool off? He knew just the spot!

Lincoln galloped at full pace towards the pool.
A place to swim, so crisp and so cool.

3, 2, 1 Jump!

Lincoln cannonballed into the pool but landed with a thump.

All the water left the pool with a splash.
The dogs nearby got an unwanted bath.

He turned to see what happened and boy were they mad.
Lincoln hung his head low and left the park feeling sad.

Cheer up Lincoln it isn't so bad.
Tomorrow is a new day, a new chance, so be glad!

You have lots of love to share, but remember you are large.
Perhaps next time the other dogs can take charge.

Lincoln felt better knowing this was true.
If he slowed things down he might make a friend or two.

The next day at the park Lincoln crept in slow.
Other dogs were playing fetch, but he decided to lay low.

Just then the dogs started to bark.

What happened? What's going on? There's an emergency at the park!

The ball is out of reach. It got stuck in the tree.

They'll never get it down. How could this be?

Lincoln saw the commotion. This is no time to act shy.

They needed someone tall, someone large and he knew just the guy!

Lincoln stretched out and grabbed the toy.

The other dogs were so happy, they jumped for joy!

The dogs allowed him to play and were no longer afraid.
Although he was large, he was so well behaved.

After hours of play it was time for a water break.
The other dogs were nervous. They knew what was at stake.

To their surprise, Lincoln passed right by the water bowls.
He didn't look down at them, just continued his stroll.

Lincoln was headed for the pipes, the fountain, the source.
It made perfect sense. It was just his size, of course!

This time every dog drank in plenty.
Onto the pool, but would it soon be empty?

Lincoln bounded toward the pool but remembered one thing.
If he made a big splash what disappointment would that bring?

He came to a screeching stop, then stepped into the water not
spilling one drop.

His friends jumped in and joined him for a float.
Some of the dogs used Lincoln for a boat!

It's a good thing Lincoln came back a second day.
Now he has new pals and is here to stay.

Lincoln learned an important lesson.

No matter how large or small,
here at the dog park there is room for all.

About Lincoln [the co-author]

Breed: Great Dane
Standing Height: 7 feet
Favorite Snack: Peanut butter
Favorite TV Channel: HGTV
Favorite Job: Participating in the neighborhood watch
Favorite Outside Activity: Sun bathing
Favorite Indoor Activity: Eating the hardwood floors
Dislikes: Commercials, Rainy Days
If Lincoln were human, he would be a lawyer or gardener.

To follow Lincoln's daily adventures, visit
his Instagram, Lincoln.Lives.Large

CPSIA information can be obtained
at www.ICGtesting.com
Printed in the USA
BVHW050609051218
534802BV00004B/29/P